I0813610

GEOFF EATON

with illustrations by DC DESIGN HOUSE INC.

BREAKWATER

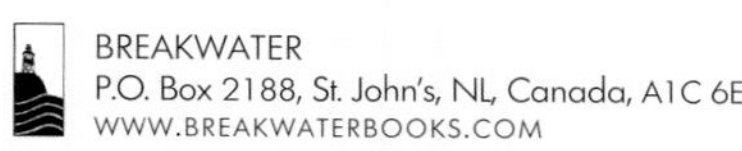
BREAKWATER
P.O. Box 2188, St. John's, NL, Canada, A1C 6E6
WWW.BREAKWATERBOOKS.COM

LIBRARY AND ARCHIVES CANADA CATALOGUING IN PUBLICATION
Eaton, Geoff, author
Six things / Geoff Eaton.
ISBN 978-1-55081-734-8
1. Conduct of life--Juvenile literature. 2. Success in children--Juvenile literature. 3. Self-actualization (Psychology)--Juvenile literature. 4. Elementary school graduates--Juvenile literature. 5. Academic achievement--Juvenile literature. I. Title.
BJ1631.E28 2018 j170.83'4 C2018-900377-4

Second Printing

We acknowledge the support of the Canada Council for the Arts, which last year invested $153 million to bring the arts to Canadians throughout the country. We acknowledge the financial support of the Government of Canada and the Government of Newfoundland and Labrador through the Department of Tourism, Culture, Industry and Innovation for our publishing activities.
PRINTED AND BOUND IN CANADA.

Canada Council for the Arts Conseil des Arts du Canada

Newfoundland Labrador

Breakwater Books is committed to choosing papers and materials for our books that help to protect our environment. To this end, this book is printed on a recycled paper that is certified by the Forest Stewardship Council®.

Adia, Mira, Kane, and Karen,
you are the four things that matter most.
Love you.

1 YOUR CHOICES MATTER, EVEN WHEN YOU'RE YOUNG.

Even though you're young, you can make a difference. And that difference could be good or bad.

Every day, the choices you make as you connect with friends (or not), work hard in school (or not), play hard after school (or not), they all matter.

This is not something to stress about, but something to be aware of. Your choices shape your life.

You will see the **RESULTS** of your choices.

2 YOU WILL SCREW-UP AND FAIL: IT'S OKAY.

Perfection is a myth you should put out of your mind now and forever. Consider being "great," not perfect.

Be a great
friend, a
great brother
or sister.
As you grow,
consider
being a great
change-maker.

Whatever your path, it will involve screwing-up. This is totally okay, especially if you learn from it. We can't learn everything from our parents and teachers; you need to learn some things on your own.

Screwing-up is a great way to LEARN.

3 YOUR GRADES IN SCHOOL AREN'T YOUR GRADES IN LIFE.

There are two important pieces here: your teachers grade your work in school, but you decide if you are satisfied with your grades. Life works the same way. Many people will grade you in life, but you decide if you have accomplished what you wanted.

Whatever your grades, As or Cs, you can accomplish awesome things.

The world is changed in big and small ways every day by people who want to make a difference.

What really matters is what you decide to do with your ENERGY and TALENT.

4

1% IS NOT 0%.

This is extra important to remember when you dream about your future. There will be people who tell you something can't be done. They'll say you only have a 1% chance.

Well 1% is still a CHANCE.

Be thankful for the naysayers. They will give you extra

energy to chase your dream. Just because something is a longshot doesn't mean you shouldn't go for it.

5 GIV'ER–DREAM IT AND DO IT!

Having a dream—big or small—is the second most important thing you will do in your life.

The most
important thing
will be what
you do with
your dreams.

Take your fear,
uncertainty, questions,
curiosity, desire,
energy—
take all of it with you—and...

Go **CHASE** your **DREAMS**!

Make it your number one priority and have a super time doing it.

6 THE MOST IMPORTANT THINGS IN LIFE AREN'T THINGS.

Some people go their whole life
and think it's about the stuff—

the awards, the toys, even the letters after their name.

Many, many years from now, when you look back on your most important accomplishments, these things will be meaningless.

The most important things in life are the **EXPERIENCES** we have and the **IMPACT** we make on others in our community and our world.

AUTHOR'S NOTE

There were times in my life when I was not expected to live. I've had cancer twice and, at one point, complications from treatment put me on life-support. I was given less than a two-percent chance of living. What's less than two?

I started my own business a year before I left university, and while working late one night, I was struck with a realization: I had been working harder than I ever had in my life, I was making less money than I ever had, yet I was happier than I'd ever been. How is this possible?

I learned that what got me going was recognizing an opportunity to make an impact and going after it—GIVIN' 'ER!

Dealing with cancer at a young age prompted me to reflect on my life, as short as it was at that point, and I can tell you the most important things we have in this life aren't *things* at all; they are the experiences we have while we are here.

I will leave you with some words of wisdom from a good friend of mine. I met him first in the movie *Pinocchio*. His name is Jiminy Cricket, and right at the end of the movie, Jiminy is bouncing on Pinocchio's shoulder and he says, "If your heart is in your dream, no request is too extreme."

Chase your dreams and have a great time doing it.

Always...

Live life. Love life.

Geoff

Geoff Eaton is a social entrepreneur, a two-time cancer survivor, and an advocate for young adults living with, through, and beyond cancer. He is the executive director of Young Adult Cancer Canada (YACC), and brings his message—live life, love life—to kids everywhere. He lives in St. John's.

Dc Design House brands better, for our team, our clients, and our place. We invest our talent, time, and passion—to collaborate and make things happen. Looking forward!